# ADVENTURE ON KLICKITAT ISLAND

## Hilary Horder Hippely

### illustrated by Barbara Upton

Baby's First Book Club®

For my son, Luke,
and for our friend and teacher,
Susan Ann Holmberg
H.H.H.


For my parents, Howard and Jean
B.U.

Copyright © This Edition 2000
Baby's First Book Club®
Bristol, PA 19007

Text copyright © 1998 by Hilary Horder Hippely
Illustrations copyright © 1998 by Barbara Upton
All rights reserved.

First published in the United States in 1999 by Dutton Children's Books,
a division of Penguin Putnam Books for Young Readers, New York, NY 10014
Designed by Semadar Megged
Printed in Hongkong
ISBN 1-58048-096-9

**O**ne dark autumn evening,
the full moon was hiding;
I heard the wind moaning
and saw the sea rising.

"It's a storm," I told Beary
    and tucked him in tight.
"That noisy old thunder
    might rumble all night.

"But with Blankie around us
    there's nothing to fear;
at least we're not out
    with the eagles and deer.

"On Klickitat Island
    just think of the rains,
now soaking the otters
    and poor baby cranes."

Then I hummed for a while
    and was closing my eyes,
when I saw Beary jump up
    and to my surprise

he reached for his jacket—
    "Someone's calling," he said.
"We can't be much help
    if we stay here in bed!"

So I snatched up our blankie
    and quick as could be
we crept down the back stairs
    and ran to the sea.

Our dinghy was waiting
   by the creaky old dock;
we climbed in together
   and rowed past the rock.

Then waves pitched us so high
   and crashed us so low,
we almost lost track of
   which way we should go.

Up ahead loomed the island.
  "Row hard," I told Bear.
"We'll make it together—
  three pulls and we're there."

We took a deep breath
  when we stepped on the sand,
clutching our blankie
  and each other's hand.

The beach seemed deserted—
  it was so hard to see.
But who had been calling
  to Beary and me?

We heard a few sniffles,
 then somebody sneezed,
and a rabbit hopped out
 from under the trees.

He waved one big paw,
 so we ran to his side.
Such a pitiful sight!
 We both almost cried.

For there in a clearing
    huddled deer, birds, and otters—
so sad and bedraggled
    and drenched with storm waters!

"We're scared," explained Rabbit,
    "to be out in this storm.
We should all stay together—
    cozy and warm.

"But our nests and our burrows
    and our caves are too small.
We can't find a home
    the right size for us all."

Then together they cried,
    they wept for so long,
that I finally yelled, "Stop it!
    So much crying is wrong.

"We've brought you our blankie—
    we'll share it with you;
it helps us feel brave
    and will help you all, too.

"But first we need shelter
    from this dark, stormy sky.
We need to build something
    to keep us all dry."

"Build?" replied Eagle.
    "I'm an excellent scout.
I'll find the best sticks
    and twigs lying about."

"I'll fetch them," cried Moose.
    "Let me help," added Deer.
"I'll also haul driftwood—
    the beach is so near."

"How about clamshells?" said Otter.
　"And seaweed and kelp?"
"How about brambles?" asked Rabbit.
　"And boulders should help."

Two bears rolled the boulders
　and piled them up high....
They built a great fireplace
　that reached toward the sky.

Then we propped and we piled
　all the driftwood we'd found,
and plugged up the holes
　from the roof to the ground.

"Rumble! Boom!" crashed the thunder,
　but now no one cared;
with so much to work on,
　how could we be scared?

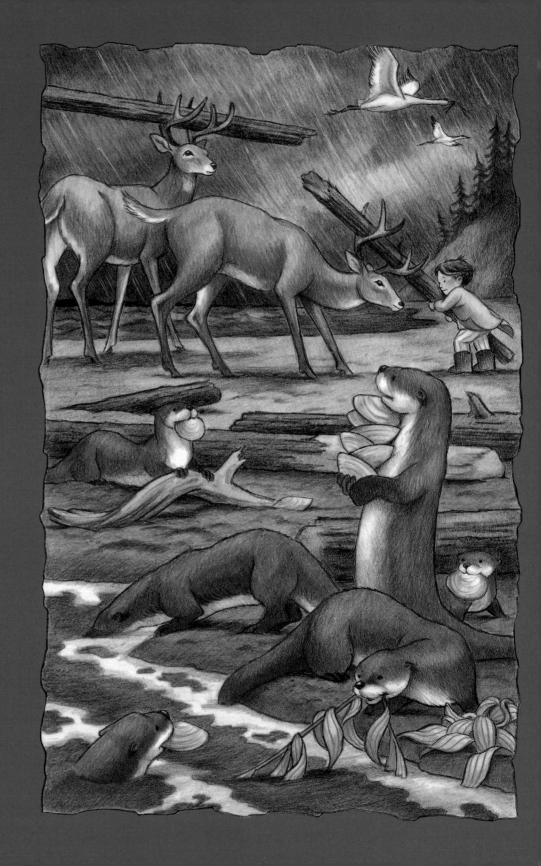

With deer hauling driftwood
and cranes helping sort,
soon standing up tall
was a Klickitat fort!

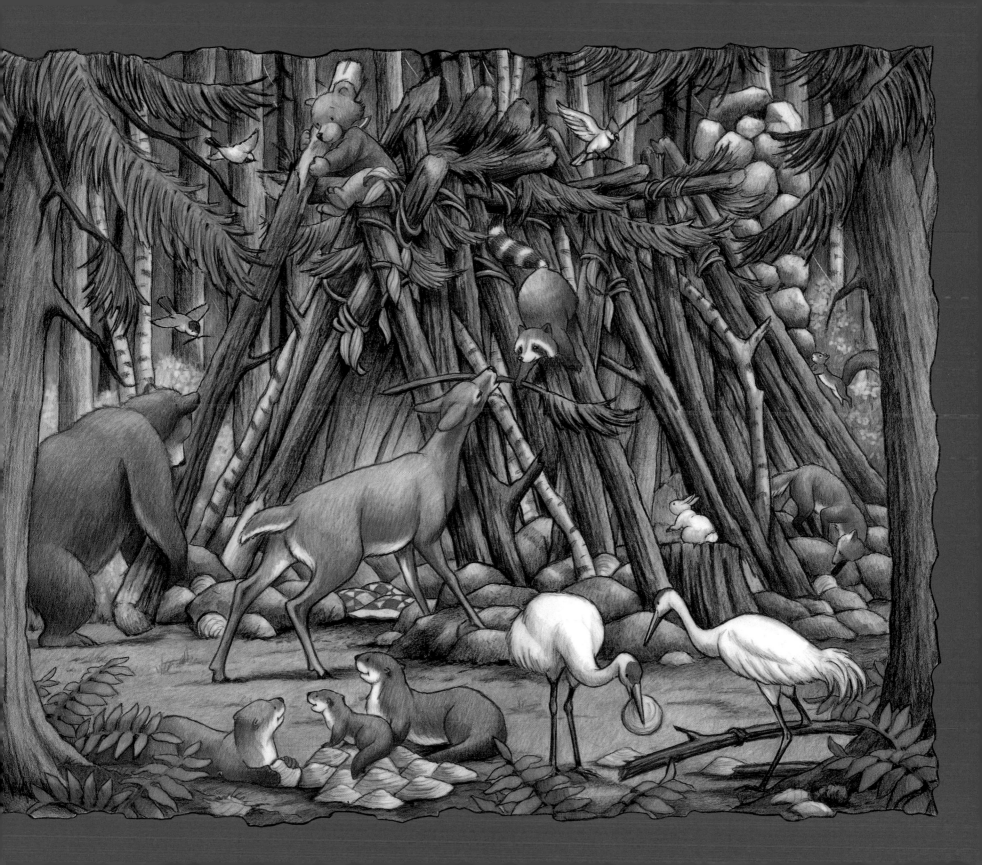

For a moment we stood
   in that terrible weather,
amazed by the home
   we had all built together.

Then Moose led a cheer—
   "Hip hooray!" we all cried,
and hurried to fill up
   the warm space inside.

"Now a story," said Rabbit.
	"It's time for a tale."
But right in the middle,
	we heard a sad wail.

There sat an otter—
	just a baby, so sweet.
"No one's sharing," he whimpered,
	"I can't cover my feet!"

We pulled and we stretched
    to give him some blankie,
but it didn't quite reach
    so Bear gave him his hanky.

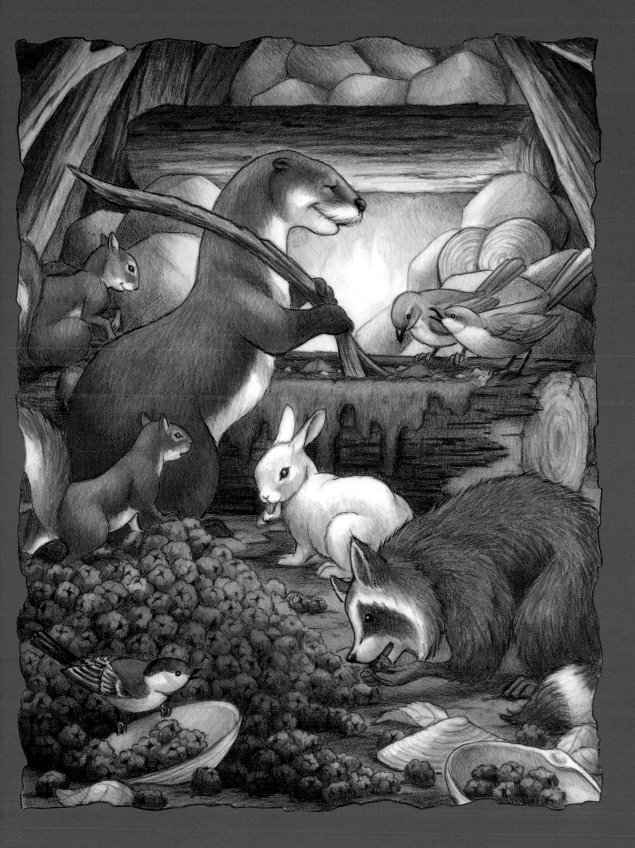

"Now I'm cozy," sighed Otter.
  "I just wish I could eat!"
So his grandma concocted
  the tastiest treat.

It was partly a cake
  and partly a soup;
we all helped ourselves
  from a long-handled scoop.

Before long we got sleepy
    by that warm fireside,
while the wind moaned and howled
    and the rain poured outside.

Soon an eagle was yawning
    by a young chickadee;
then the whole clan was snoring
    except Beary and me.

"Sleep tight," I told Beary,
    as I gave him a hug.
"We'll stay here till morning,
    safe, warm, and snug."

But the storm must have broken
    as we both lay there dreaming.
When we opened our eyes,
    the full moon was gleaming.

We tiptoed away
    so our friends wouldn't wake,
and we rowed the dark sea—
    now as still as a lake.

We woke in the morning,
    our room full of light,
but we know where to go
    the next dark, stormy night!